LEGENDS OF THE AMERICAS

VOLADORES

Patricia Petersen ◆ Illustrated by Sheli Petersen

PETER BEDRICK BOOKS

S

McGraw-Hill
Children's Publishing
A Division of The McGraw-Hill Companies

This edition published in the United States in 2002
by Peter Bedricks Books, an imprint of
McGraw-Hill Children's Publishing,
A Division of The McGraw-Hill Companies
8787 Orion Place
Columbus, OH 43240

www.MHkids.com

ISBN 1-57768-972-0

Copyright © 2002 by Laredo Publishing Co.
9400 Lloydcrest Drive Beverly Hills, CA 90210

1 2 3 4 5 6 7 8 9 10 LAR 06 05 04 03 02 01

LEGENDS OF THE AMERICAS SERIES
In the same series:
Gray Feather and the Big Dog

Library of Congress Cataloging-in-Publication Data
Petersen, Patricia, 1945-
   Voladores/Patricia Petersen; illustrated by Sheli Petersen.
        p. cm. -- (Legends of the Americas)
   Summary: When Water and Volcano become jealous of the
people's devotion to Sun, they cause chaos which can only be
overcome by Wind, but only one small boy is willing to try to reach
Wind to ask for his help.
   ISBN 1-57768-972-0
   1. Indians of Mexico--Folklore. 2. Flying dance--Mexico--Folklore.
[1. Indians of Mexico--Folklore. 2. Flying dance. 3. Folklore--
Mexico.] 1. Petersen, Sheli, 1969-ill. II. Title. III. Series.

F1219.3.D2 P44 2002
398.2'089'97--dc 21
[Fic]   2001043659

Printed and bound in China

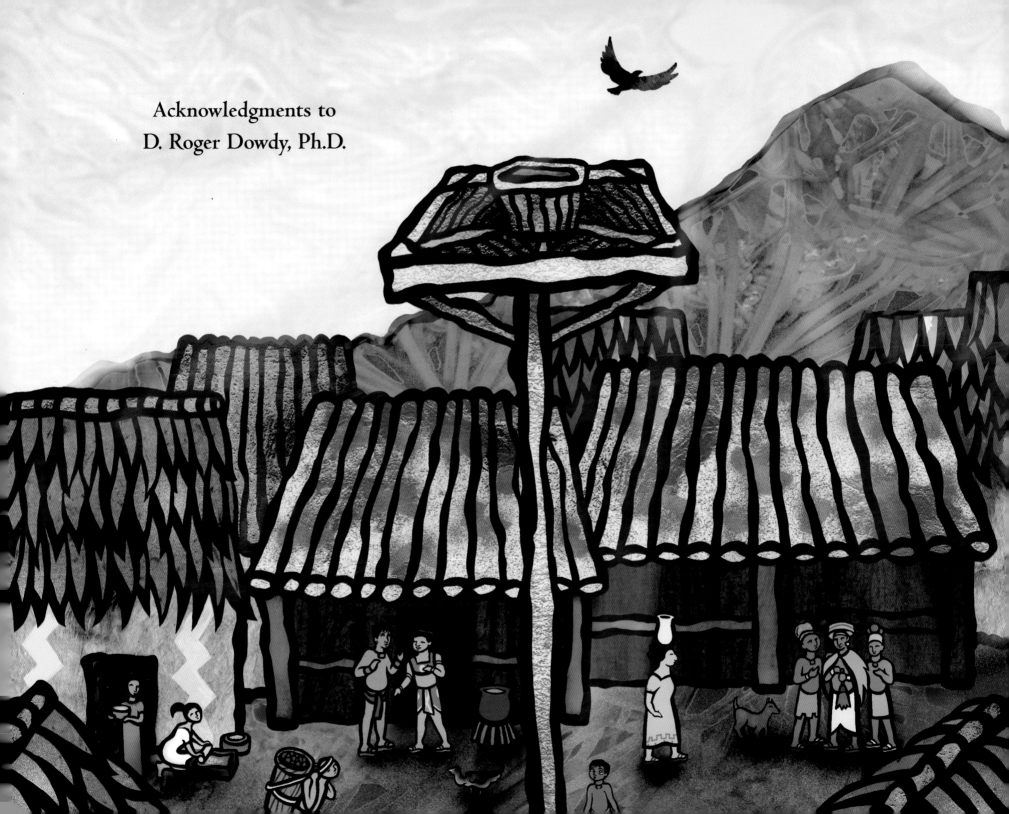

Acknowledgments to
D. Roger Dowdy, Ph.D.

In the time before the old ways were forgotten, chosen men flew in honor of the Sun. These men were called the voladores. On certain feasts of the year, they climbed the tallest pole in the town square to seek the Sun's promise of joy and good harvest. The whole village watched as the voladores rose in solemn flight. To the sound of the flute, they flew across the sky until noon. Then they came back to earth with the Sun's blessing.

In the village of the voladores lived a boy named Tigre. Tigre loved to watch his Uncle Teo and the other voladores put on their wings while his Uncle Quiche played the flute.

6

When Tigre was old enough, his uncles took him to
the forest. Uncle Quiche had him choose a sapling with which
to make his very own flute, and Uncle Teo helped him gather
brightly colored feathers to make his own pair of wings. As soon as
Tigre felt the little wings on his shoulders, he knew someday he, too,
would fly with the voladores. He tried hard to be patient while
Uncle Quiche taught him to play the flute. But as soon as Tigre
finished playing, he was off to the hillside to watch
the eagle and learn his ways.

In those days Tigre and his people were happy. The animals were their friends, and they spoke to the birds as brothers. The Sun bathed them in its warm light and made the corn flourish in their fields. They were never hungry nor afraid.

"But one day the volcano awoke from a long sleep. He saw the voladores returning from their flight and began to envy the favor they enjoyed with the Sun. The volcano scowled and searched the clouds that circled his rim for his cousin, the rain god. "Look how these people love the Sun," he told the rain god. "We are as important as he, but no one worships us."

"You're right," said the rain god. "But what can we do? We can't fight the Sun. He's too strong for us."

"If we can't defeat the Sun, we will destroy his friends, the voladores. For twenty days, I will shake the earth and cover it with lava and smoke. When the voladores try to fly, I will singe their wings and make them fall to the ground. Then they will think the Sun is angry and is withholding his blessing."

The rain god agreed. "Then, for twenty days, I will make rain. Water will cover the earth and sky. The people will think the Sun has forgotten them. Then they will learn to honor us."

It all happened as the volcano said it would. For twenty days, the earth rumbled and shook. The sky was black with smoke, and people hid in their huts. But the voladores knew what to do. They were going to fly and ask the Sun for help.

The voladores climbed the tall pole and rose in flight, hoping to ask the Sun to chase away the smoke. One by one, they flew over the volcano. As soon as the voladores appeared above his rim, the volcano belched angry flames that singed their wings. He laughed as the voladores fell helplessly to the ground. The men were no match for the volcano's power.

After twenty days, the volcano was silent. Then the rain god kept his vow to cause hardship for Tigre's people. For the next twenty days, water covered both land and sky.

The nearby lake overflowed from its banks. Fish swam in the treetops. Mud choked the fields and ruined the corn.

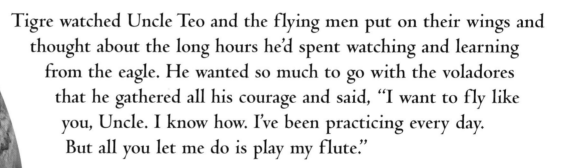

Tigre watched Uncle Teo and the flying men put on their wings and thought about the long hours he'd spent watching and learning from the eagle. He wanted so much to go with the voladores that he gathered all his courage and said, "I want to fly like you, Uncle. I know how. I've been practicing every day. But all you let me do is play my flute."

Uncle Teo put his hand on Tigre's shoulder. "One day you'll be glad of your flute. It may be more useful than your wings." His uncle smiled. "Now play, so we can fly well."

Once more, Teo and the voladores climbed the tall pole, ready to fly to ask the Sun for help. But the rain god had gathered every cloud in the sky. Water poured down on the voladores, soaking their beautiful feathers. Their wings grew so heavy with rain, they fell into the newly formed lake.

When the rain finally stopped, the sky remained dark and cloudy. Though the whole village watched the horizon, the Sun did not appear. Tigre and his people were hungry and cold. Some thought the Sun was angry. Others thought the Sun had gone to live in a far away land.

The village elders held a meeting. After considering the matter for some time, the oldest and wisest of the elders said, "Someone must go to the house of the wind and ask him to sweep away the clouds. Only with his help can the Sun return. Send for the voladores so we may choose the bravest of them."

But the bravest of them was Uncle Teo, who lay sick in bed after falling into the lake. The voladores listened to the elders in silence. None of them dared to undertake such a dangerous task.

No one knew that Tigre had witnessed the entire meeting from high in the rafters. Suddenly the boy cried, "My Uncle Teo cannot fly because he is sick. So I will go instead."

21

The elders laughed. "Do I hear a cricket chirping on the roof?" asked one.

Some of the men spied Tigre hiding in the thatch and brought him down. "Come here," said the wise one. "What do you know of flying?"

"I practice every day with the wings Uncle Teo made me. I knew that someday I would take my place in the sky."

"A boy as small as you must have wings like a hummingbird," laughed the elder. "It is a long and dangerous journey to the house of the wind god. Who will go with you?"

"I will ask my brother, the eagle, to guide me. He flies higher and sees beyond the horizon."

So it was decided that Tigre would be the newest and youngest of the voladores. At dawn, Tigre went to the village square and played a sad and beautiful song on his flute. As soon as he had finished, he tucked the flute in his belt and began to climb to the top of the pole. When he reached the platform, he waited until he felt the wind stir his feathers, and he dove into the air.

Soon he was flying beside the eagle as he had dreamed he would. They flew all day and all night. When Tigre was tired, the eagle carried him. At last, they arrived at the house of the wind god.

"What do you want?" asked the wind god, angrily. "Can't you see I'm sleeping?"

Tigre bowed. "Sir, for many years my people have honored the Sun, and he smiled on us. Our corn grew tall and sweet. Our people were happy. But now a great cloud hangs over our land. The people are hungry and afraid. They think the Sun has forgotten them."

The wind god frowned. "I am very strong. But the Sun is stronger still. If he has forgotten you, I can do nothing."

"But, sir! You're the only one who can help us," Tigre pleaded, "If you sweep away the clouds…"

"And what will a small boy give for such a big favor?"

Tigre thought for a moment. "I have only the flute Uncle Quiche made me. Its music is very beautiful."

"Well, play it for me," said the wind god, beginning to lose his patience.

Tigre played the most beautiful song he knew. He saw the wind god frown and turn away as a servant brought his breakfast, but Tigre kept playing. When he had finished, Tigre went slowly to the wind god's table.

"What do you want now?" asked the wind god, wiping his mouth.

"I would like to know your answer, please," said Tigre.

The wind god laughed at the boy's courage. "All right. Give me your flute and I'll grant your wish. Now, go." The wind god scowled, but he was secretly pleased with his bargain.

Tigre was sad to lose his flute, but he gave it to the wind knowing that it would buy the god's help and save his people. Then Tigre flew home with the eagle by his side.

The next morning, when his wings came to rest in the square, Tigre found all the people waiting, including Uncle Teo and Uncle Quiche. The Sun shone brightly on the horizon and not a cloud could be seen. The rain god and the volcano could only sulk in silence. Tigre was very tired but his heart was content. His people were happy again. They could look forward to a good harvest and would continue to honor their friend, the Sun. Best of all, Tigre saw the pride in Uncle Teo's eyes and knew he had earned his place among the voladores.

0|3 5|04   8-07-04 05